LAS VEGAS
RAIDERS

BY JOSH ANDERSON

Stride

An Imprint of The Child's World®

childsworld.com

The Child's World

childsworld.com

Published by The Child's World®
800-599-READ • www.childsworld.com

ISBN Information
9781503857827 (Reinforced Library Binding)
9781503860629 (Portable Document Format)
9781503861985 (Online Multi-user eBook)
9781503863347 (Electronic Publication)

LCCN 2021952687

Printed in the United States of America

TABLE OF CONTENTS

GO RAIDERS!

The Las Vegas Raiders compete in the National Football **League's** (NFL's) American Football Conference (AFC). They play in the AFC West **division**, along with the Denver Broncos, Kansas City Chiefs, and Los Angeles Chargers. The Raiders had their greatest success in the late 1970s and early 1980s. From 1976 to 1983, the Raiders won the **Super Bowl** three times. Let's learn more about the Raiders!

AFC WEST DIVISION

Denver Broncos

Kansas City Chiefs

Las Vegas Raiders

Los Angeles Chargers

THE RAIDERS STARTED 2021 WITH A BANG, WINNING THEIR FIRST THREE GAMES OF THE SEASON.

BECOMING THE RAIDERS

The Oakland Raiders began play in 1960 as a member of the American Football League (AFL). The Raiders joined the NFL when the AFL and NFL combined in 1970. The team moved to Los Angeles in 1982, then back to Oakland in 1995. In 2020, the Raiders began play in their new home city of Las Vegas, Nevada. They're the first NFL football team ever to make its home in Las Vegas.

RAIDERS LINEBACKER TED HENDRICKS (CENTER) STOOD 6 FEET, 7 INCHES (201 CM) TALL AND WAS NICKNAMED "THE MAD STORK."

BY THE NUMBERS

The Raiders have won **THREE** Super Bowls.

16 division titles for the Raiders

479 points scored by the team in 2000— a Raiders record!

13 wins for the Raiders in 1976

DEREK CARR HAS STARTED EVERY GAME HE'S EVER PLAYED FOR THE RAIDERS.

ALLEGIANT STADIUM'S ROOF WAS DESIGNED TO LET IN LIGHT FROM THE BRIGHT LAS VEGAS SUNSHINE.

Since 2020, the Raiders have played their home games at Allegiant **Stadium**. The stadium can hold 65,000 Raiders fans on game days. Allegiant Stadium has been nicknamed the "Death Star" for its resemblance to the ship of the same name in the *Star Wars* movies. Near the North End Zone, there is a huge torch that stays lit in honor of former team owner Al Davis. The torch is the largest 3D-printed object in the world.

We're Famous!

Former Raiders head coach John Madden brought the Raiders to the **playoffs** eight times. He also led them to a Super Bowl victory. He's the name behind the *Madden NFL* video game franchise from EA Sports. Since 1988, the game has delighted football fans. Even NFL players look forward to seeing how their skills are rated when the game is released each year.

UNIFORM

BLACK

WHITE

Truly Weird

The Raiders had an incredible comeback in a 1968 game against the New York Jets, but half the country missed the action! When the high-scoring game went longer than expected, television network NBC cut away from the game in the eastern United States to show the film *Heidi*. Football fans still talk about missing out on the Raiders' two last-minute **touchdowns** in the "*Heidi* Game."

Alternate Jersey

Sometimes teams wear an alternate jersey that is different from their home and away jerseys. It might be a bright color or have a unique theme. The Raiders wore their white and silver jerseys for a 2020 game against the Los Angeles Chargers. The different look proved lucky for Las Vegas—they won the game 31–26.

RAIDERS FANS SHOW SUPPORT FOR THEIR FAVORITE TEAM WITH CREATIVE MASKS AND COSTUMES.

TEAM SPIRIT

Going to a game at Allegiant Stadium can be a blast! "Raider Nation" is considered one of the most passionate fan bases in all of sports. Many fans wear masks or paint their faces silver and black when they come to root on the team. The team's cheerleaders, the Raiderettes, entertain the fans at every home game. They're joined by Raider Rusher, the team's mascot. He's a costumed Raiders football player who wears the number 1 on his jersey. Fans who are hungry have plenty of great options at the stadium. The loaded asada nachos are a tasty treat meant to be shared with friends!

RAIDER RUSHER

Tim Brown
Wide Receiver | 1988–2003

Brown's 14,934 career receiving yards rank seventh in NFL history. His 100 career receiving touchdowns rank ninth. From 1993 to 2001, Brown registered nine consecutive 1,000–receiving yards seasons. He was chosen for nine **Pro Bowls** and is a member of the Pro Football **Hall of Fame**.

Howie Long
Defensive End | 1981–1993

Long helped anchor the defense for the Raiders team that won Super Bowl 18 after the 1983 season. Although **sacks** were not an official statistic until 1982, he registered 91.5 in his career. Long was chosen for eight Pro Bowls. He is a member of the Pro Football Hall of Fame.

Ken Stabler
Quarterback | 1970–1979

Stabler was named the NFL's **Most Valuable Player** (MVP) in 1974. That year, he led the NFL with 26 touchdown passes. Stabler helped lead the Raiders to victory in Super Bowl 11. His 19,078 passing yards for the Raiders are second in team history. He was inducted into the Pro Football Hall of Fame in 2016.

Gene Upshaw
Offensive Guard | 1967–1981

Upshaw started in 24 playoff games during his career and won 15 of them. He helped lead the Raiders to two Super Bowl victories. Upshaw was chosen for seven Pro Bowls and is a member of the Pro Football Hall of Fame. He was picked for the NFL's 100th Anniversary All-Time Team.

JANUARY 25, 1981

The Raiders win Super Bowl 15 by defeating the Philadelphia Eagles 27–10.

In Super Bowl 18, the Raiders defeat the Washington Football Team 38–9.

JANUARY 22, 1984

BIG DAYS

MAY 9, 2014

With a second round pick in the 2014 NFL Draft, the Raiders select quarterback Derek Carr.

The Raiders play in their first playoff game in 14 seasons.

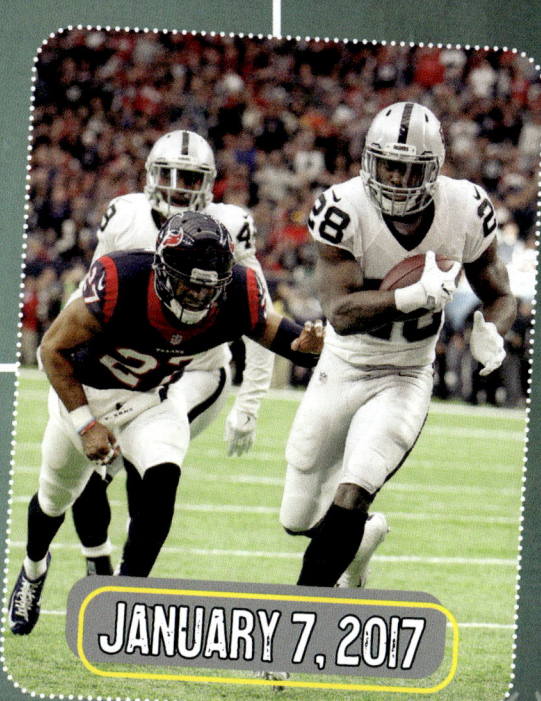

JANUARY 7, 2017

MODERN-DAY MARVELS

Davante Adams
Wide Receiver | Debut: 2022

Adams played his first eight seasons for the Green Bay Packers. He led the league in 2020 with 18 touchdown catches. Adams was selected for the Pro Bowl each year from 2017 through 2021. No player in the league caught more touchdowns between 2016 and 2021. Adams is shown here in his old Packers uniform.

Derek Carr
Quarterback | Debut: 2014

Carr is the Raiders' all-time leader in passing yards with 31,700 and passing touchdowns with 193. He had 24 fourth-quarter comebacks in his first eight seasons. No other player in NFL history has achieved that feat. He's been chosen for the Pro Bowl three times.

Maxx Crosby
Defensive End | Debut: 2019

Crosby played in college at Eastern Michigan University. The Raiders selected him with a fourth-round pick in the 2019 NFL Draft. Crosby led the Raiders in sacks during the first two seasons of his career. He was only the second Raider to ever record at least ten sacks as a **rookie**.

Darren Waller
Tight End | Debut: 2018

Waller had back-to-back 1,000-yard seasons in 2019 and 2020. His 107 catches in 2020 broke a Raiders' single-season record. During one game in 2020, Waller totaled 200 receiving yards. That's only 14 yards short of the single-game record for a tight end. Waller was also chosen for his first Pro Bowl in 2020.

MARCUS ALLEN RUSHED FOR 8,545 YARDS AND 79 TOUCHDOWNS AS A RAIDER.

MARCUS ALLEN

Allen ranks third all-time with 123 rushing touchdowns for his career. He also ranks 14th all-time with 12,243 career rushing yards. Allen was chosen as the NFL's MVP after the 1985 season when he rushed for 1,759 yards and 11 touchdowns. He was also named MVP of Super Bowl 18. In the game, Allen rushed for 191 yards and two touchdowns. He's a member of the Pro Football Hall of Fame.

FAN FAVORITE

Bo Jackson–Running Back
1987–1990

Although he only played football for four seasons, Jackson is an iconic member of the Raiders and a favorite of many NFL fans. Jackson was not only an incredible running back, he was also an All-Star in Major League Baseball. He hit 141 home runs in eight seasons.

THE BIG GAME

JANUARY 9, 1977 – SUPER BOWL II

The Raiders earned their second-ever trip to the Super Bowl after finishing the 1976 season with a 13–1 record. Their opponents in the big game were the Minnesota Vikings. The Vikings were led by future Hall of Fame quarterback Fran Tarkenton. But the Raiders defense held the Vikings scoreless for nearly three quarters as they built a 19–0 lead. The Raiders finished the game with a 32–14 victory. Wide receiver Fred Biletnikoff finished the game with 79 receiving yards and was named MVP.

THE AWARD FOR THE YEAR'S MOST OUTSTANDING RECEIVER IN COLLEGE FOOTBALL IS NAMED FOR FRED BILETNIKOFF.

TOM FLORES COACHED THE RAIDERS TO TWO SUPER BOWL VICTORIES.

AMAZING FEATS

4,804 Passing Yards

In 2021 by
QUARTERBACK
Derek Carr

16 Rushing Touchdowns

In 1975 by
RUNNING BACK
Pete Banaszak

107 Catches

In 2020 by
TIGHT END
Darren Waller

16 Receiving Touchdowns

In 1963 by
WIDE RECEIVER
Art Powell

ALL-TIME BEST

PASSING YARDS

Derek Carr
31,700*

Ken Stabler
19,078

Rich Gannon
17,585

RUSHING YARDS

Marcus Allen
8,545

Mark van Eeghen
5,907

Clem Daniels
5,103

RECEIVING YARDS

Tim Brown
14,734

Fred Biletnikoff
8,974

Cliff Branch
8,685

SACKS**

Greg Townsend
107.5

Howie Long
91.5

Ben Davidson
62

SCORING

Sebastian Janikowski
1,799

George Blanda
863

Chris Bahr
817

INTERCEPTIONS

Willie Brown
39

Lester Hayes
39

Terry McDaniel
34

*as of 2021
**unofficial before 1982

DEFENSIVE END GREG TOWNSEND PLAYED 12 SEASONS FOR THE RAIDERS.

GLOSSARY

division (dih-VIZSH-un): a group of teams within the NFL who play each other more frequently and compete for the best record

Hall of Fame (HAHL of FAYM): a museum in Canton, Ohio, that honors the best players in NFL history

league (LEEG): an organization of sports teams that compete against each other

Most Valuable Player (MOHST VAL-yuh-bul PLAY-uhr): a yearly award given to the top player in the NFL

playoffs (PLAY-ahfs): a series of games played after the regular season that decides which two teams play in the Super Bowl

Pro Bowl (PRO BOWL): the NFL's All-Star game, where the best players in the league compete

rookie (RUH-kee): a player playing in his first season

sack (SAK): when a quarterback is tackled behind the line of scrimmage before he can throw the ball

stadium (STAY-dee-uhm): a building with a field and seats for fans where teams play

Super Bowl (SOO-puhr BOWL): the championship game of the NFL, played between the winners of the AFC and the NFC

touchdown (TUTCH-down): a play in which the ball is brought into the other team's end zone, resulting in six points

FIND OUT MORE

IN THE LIBRARY

Bulgar, Beth and Mark Bechtel. *My First Book of Football*.
New York, NY: Time Inc. Books, 2015.

Jacobs, Greg. *The Everything Kids' Football Book, 7th Edition*.
Avon, MA: Adams Media, 2021.

Sports Illustrated Kids. *The Greatest Football Teams of All Time*.
New York, NY: Time Inc. Books, 2018.

Wyler, Zach. *Oakland Raiders*. New York, NY: AV2 Books, 2020.

ON THE WEB

Visit our website for links about the Las Vegas Raiders:
childsworld.com/links

Note to parents, teachers, and librarians: We routinely verify our web
links to make sure they are safe and active sites. Encourage your
readers to check them out!

INDEX

ABOUT THE AUTHOR

Josh Anderson has published over 50 books for children and young adults. His two boys are the greatest joys in his life. Hobbies include coaching his sons in youth basketball, no-holds-barred games of Apples to Apples, and taking long family walks. His favorite NFL team is a secret he'll never share!